Father and Son, Honey hunt has begun!

Shelly May

Me and my dad bear
Had run out of honey.
The last tiny drop
Went into dad's tummy.

We had to get more
Before we got hungry
So we climbed up a hill
To look for the best honey.

We surveyed the scene
From the top of the hill,
But we slipped and fell down
Just like Jack and Jill.

We slid off the cliff
And flew into the sky.
"No honey here," said an eagle,
"And bears cannot fly!"

Me and dad fell swiftly,
Landing see in a lake,
"No honey here," said the fish,
"You made a mistake."

We met a kind beaver
Who was building a dam.
"I've seen no honey," he said,
"But search all you can."

Walking into the forest
Me and dad met a moose.
We'd ask him or help,
We had nothing to lose.

We three shared a campfire.
I asked, "Have you seen any bees?"
"You should talk to the squirrels,
They live in the trees."

The moose took me and dad
Across the stream on his back
To seek out the squirrels,
We were on the right track.

Me and dad climbed a tree
To ask squirrels what they think.
"We haven't see honey bees,
You should talk to the lynx."

The lynx looked surprised
To see bears on his perch,
"I don't know where honey is,
But good luck with your search."

Me and dad met a wolf pack
Camped under a tree.
One said, "Try some cherries,
You don't have to brave bees."

We saw a large python
Curled around a wood pile.
The snake made me nervous,
I hid behind dad awhile.

A fox invited me and dad
To visit in his dens,
But the holes were too small
And we got stuck instead.

Oh, what a surprise
When me and dad struggled free,
We saw lots o hives
Swarming with bees.

The bees all buzzed happily,
"Please share our honey."
So, me and dad filled our pot
And our big fat bear tummies.